# MISSING!

## Flame

### Have you seen this kitten?

Flame is a magic kitten of royal blood, missing from his own world.
His uncle, Ebony, is very keen that he is found quickly.
Flame may be hard to spot as he often appears in a
variety of fluffy kitten colours but you can recognize him
by his big emerald eyes and whiskers that crackle with magic!

He is believed to be looking for a young friend to take care of him.

### Could it be you?

If you find this very special kitten please let Ebony,
ruler of the Lion Throne, know.

Sue Bentley's books for children often include animals or fairies. She lives in Northampton and enjoys reading, going to the cinema, and sitting watching the frogs and newts in her garden pond. If she hadn't been a writer she would probably have been a skydiver or brain surgeon. The main reason she writes is that she can drink pots and pots of tea while she's typing. She has met and owned many cats and each one has brought a special sort of magic to her life.

# Magic Kitten

## Firelight Friends

# SUE BENTLEY

## Illustrated by Angela Swan

**PUFFIN**

*To Sophie – a nervous neighbourly kitty*

PUFFIN BOOKS

Published by the Penguin Group
Penguin Books Ltd, 80 Strand, London WC2R 0RL, England
Penguin Group (USA) Inc., 375 Hudson Street, New York, New York 10014, USA
Penguin Group (Canada), 90 Eglinton Avenue East, Suite 700, Toronto, Ontario, Canada M4P 2Y3
(a division of Pearson Penguin Canada Inc.)
Penguin Ireland, 25 St Stephen's Green, Dublin 2, Ireland (a division of Penguin Books Ltd)
Penguin Group (Australia), 250 Camberwell Road, Camberwell, Victoria 3124, Australia
(a division of Pearson Australia Group Pty Ltd)
Penguin Books India Pvt Ltd, 11 Community Centre, Panchsheel Park,
New Delhi – 110 017, India
Penguin Group (NZ), 67 Apollo Drive, Rosedale, North Shore 0632, New Zealand
(a division of Pearson New Zealand Ltd)
Penguin Books (South Africa) (Pty) Ltd, 24 Sturdee Avenue, Rosebank,
Johannesburg 2196, South Africa

Penguin Books Ltd, Registered Offices: 80 Strand, London WC2R 0RL, England

puffinbooks.com

First published 2007
3

Text copyright © Susan Bentley, 2007
Illustrations copyright © Angela Swan, 2007
All rights reserved

The moral right of the author and illustrator has been asserted

Set in Bembo
Typeset by Palimpsest Book Production Limited, Grangemouth, Stirlingshire
Made and printed in England by Clays Ltd, St Ives plc

Except in the United States of America, this book is sold subject to the condition
that it shall not, by way of trade or otherwise, be lent, re-sold, hired out, or otherwise
circulated without the publisher's prior consent in any form of binding or cover other
than that in which it is published and without a similar condition including this condition
being imposed on the subsequent purchaser

British Library Cataloguing in Publication Data
A CIP catalogue record for this book is available from the British Library

ISBN: 978-0-141-32199-8

www.greenpenguin.co.uk

Mixed Sources
Product group from well-managed
forests and other controlled sources
www.fsc.org Cert no. SA-COC-1592
© 1996 Forest Stewardship Council

Penguin Books is committed to a sustainable future
for our business, our readers and our planet.
The book in your hands is made from paper
certified by the Forest Stewardship Council.

# Prologue

'Uncle Ebony!' gasped the young white lion as an enormous adult lion appeared on a nearby ridge. There was a flash of dazzling white light, and sparkles sprinkled the ground where the young white lion had stood. There now crouched a tiny kitten with fluffy white fur and four black-tipped paws.

Flame's tiny kitten body trembled as

he edged slowly backwards towards a grove of thorn trees. He could hear Ebony's angry roar and imagined his fierce, ice-cold eyes.

Suddenly a huge paw, almost as big as Flame's entire body, reached out from the deep shade and scooped him up. Flame gave a whine of terror and laid his ears back. This was it. One of his uncle's spies had found him!

But instead of being grabbed by the scruff of his neck and dragged out into the open, he found himself being swept further back into the safety of the trees. An old grey lion looked down at him.

'Cirrus! Thank you, old friend,' Flame mewed gratefully.

Cirrus bowed his head respectfully. 'I am glad to see you again, Prince Flame.

But it is still not safe for you to stay. Ebony is determined to take the Lion Throne from you. He will never stop searching for you.'

Flame's bright emerald eyes sparked with anger. 'This kingdom is mine by right! Perhaps I should face my uncle for it now!'

The old lion's worn teeth showed in a smile. 'Bravely said, but Ebony is still too strong for you. Use this disguise and go back to the other world to hide.'

Flame nodded. 'I will, but only until my powers are stronger. Then I will return to overthrow Ebony and his rule will end!'

'May that be soon, my prince,' Cirrus rumbled with pride and affection.

Above them both, on the high ridge, Ebony slowly turned his enormous head and his mouth opened in a terrifying roar. He leapt down and began charging towards the thorn trees, his mighty paws eating up the dusty ground.

'He knows you're here! Go now. Save yourself,' Cirrus urged.

Sparks ignited in Flame's white fur as he felt the power building inside him. His four black-tipped paws flexed and he gave a tiny mew as he felt himself falling. Falling . . .

# Chapter
# *ONE*

'I can't believe I'm finally here. I've been looking forward to summer camp for so long!' Kara Parkes said excitedly, as she hugged her mum and dad goodbye.

'Now you have a great time and make lots of new friends,' Mrs Parkes said, smiling. 'And try not to worry about Amber.'

Amber was Kara's pony. Kara had
been riding her when a fox had run
across the pony's path and she had
reared up in fright. Although Kara had
been thrown she wasn't hurt, but
Amber had strained her leg.

'OK, Mum,' Kara said, feeling an
unwelcome stab of guilt for leaving
Amber by herself.

Her dad seemed to know what she

was thinking. 'We'll make sure that Amber gets lots of extra fuss. You just concentrate on enjoying yourself,' Mr Parkes said, ruffling his daughter's sandy, shoulder-length hair.

Kara smiled at him. 'Thanks, Dad. Will you give her a hug from me every single day? And let me know what the vet says when he's checked on her leg?'

'Sure thing!' her dad promised.

Kara waved as her parents got into their car and drove off down the steep winding road. 'Bye! See you in two weeks,' she called.

Clouds passing overhead made shadows on the green slopes of the Kerry Mountains. When Kara couldn't see the car any more, she turned and went towards Torc House where a big sign over the door read 'TH Adventure Holidays'. As she went inside and wandered upstairs towards the girls' dormitories, sounds of talking and laughter floated down towards her.

Kara went slowly, trying to remember the way from when she had been shown round earlier. She had almost reached the dorms when a girl came dashing towards her. She was small and slim, with silky blonde hair and a pretty face. 'Are you in Starlings?' she asked.

Kara nodded, remembering how excited she had been at home to tear open the letter from TH Adventure Holidays and find out exactly which dorm she was going to be in.

'Me too. I think we're in here,' the girl said, pushing open the nearest door.

'Quick, let's get in! I'm Felicity, by the way.'

'Hi . . . er, I'm Kara,' Kara said, blinking in surprise as Felicity virtually hauled her into the room. 'What's the hurry?'

'Duh! Don't you *want* to get the best beds?' Felicity leapt across the room and jumped straight on to one of two beds near the window. 'This is mine. You can have the one next to me!'

Kara looked round the small room with its three identical beds and chests of drawers. The cheerful patterned rug matched the curtains and there was a comfy chair, with a patchwork cushion, in one corner. Three suitcases were piled on the rug. Kara's suitcase, which her dad had brought upstairs for her, was on the bottom.

Kara spotted a bed by itself against the wall. 'I think I'd rather have this one,' she decided, going over to sit on it.

'Please yourself,' Felicity murmured, flicking back her long hair. She flounced off her bed and began unfastening her suitcases.

'I'm glad to see that you're settling in, girls,' called a cheerful voice from the doorway.

Kara turned to see a tall woman with curly brown hair, wearing a tomato-red T-shirt, with 'TH Adventure Holidays' printed on it. It was Miss Cross, the activities organizer.

Miss Cross smiled. 'I've just found your other dorm-mate looking a bit lost. Come in, dear,' she said, beckoning to someone behind her. 'You'll be sharing with Kara and Felicity.'

A rather large, lumpy girl stepped into the room and stood looking down at the floor.

'This is Cherry Bradford, girls,' Miss Cross announced. 'I'm sure you'll soon all make friends. Remember to listen for the bell and come downstairs for tea. See you all later!'

'Cherry!' Felicity spluttered as soon as

Miss Cross had gone. 'Did you ever hear such a daft name? And how old are you?' she asked suspiciously. 'You can't come to this camp if you're more than twelve.'

Cherry shuffled her feet and went bright pink. 'I'm ten and three quarters. Mum says I'm big for my age.'

Kara smiled at Cherry, wishing that Felicity would shut up. 'It's a really unusual name. I bet people always remember it,' she said.

Cherry shot Kara a grateful look. 'My mum had a craving for cherries when she was pregnant. So she called me Cherry when I was born,' she said quietly.

'Oh, well, it could have been worse. It's lucky she didn't go bonkers on pineapples!' Kara joked.

Cherry's eyes crinkled and she started
laughing. Kara joined in.

'What's so funny? I don't get it,'
Felicity said.

'Cherry could have been called
Pineapple!' Kara explained, laughing
even harder.

Felicity looked blank. 'That's stupid! I

think you're fibbing. I bet you're laughing at me. This is the first time I've been away from home, so you should be extra nice to me instead of picking on me!'

Kara was surprised to see tears in Felicity's blue eyes. She decided to make a big effort to like her, even if Felicity did act more like a spoilt four-year-old. 'We weren't picking on you, honest,' she said.

'No, we weren't,' Cherry agreed. She fished about in her jean-jacket pocket for a bar of chocolate. After breaking it into three bits, she gave some to Kara and Felicity.

'Thanks,' Kara said, nibbling her piece.

Felicity handed her chocolate back to Cherry. 'I don't eat sweets,' she sniffled.

'They're bad for your teeth. Anyway, it's against the rules to keep food in the dorm.'

Cherry put Felicity's piece of chocolate into her mouth and held up her empty hands. 'Well, I haven't *got* any food now, have I?'

Kara bit back a grin.

Felicity glared at them both and then went back to her unpacking. She took a small threadbare teddy out of her case and gave it a hug. 'Don't either of you dare touch Marvin,' she warned, propping the teddy against her pillows. 'I've had him since I was a baby and I can't go to sleep without him.'

Just then, a bell rang somewhere in the building.

'Teatime!' Felicity jumped off her bed

and shot towards the door. 'Come on, you two!'

Cherry paused in the open doorway. 'But shouldn't we wait for K–' she began.

'I'll only be a minute. I just want to put my trainers on,' Kara said.

'She can follow us. Come on,' Felicity urged, dragging Cherry outside.

Kara's heart sank as she wondered how she was going to put up with Felicity's bossiness. She fished her trainers out of her case and then sat down by her bed on the rug to take off her sandals.

But then suddenly a flash of bright white light filled the room.

'Oh!' Kara gasped, blinded for a moment.

A crackling sound just like electricity came from the comfy chair across the room. Blinking hard, Kara peered slowly over her bed and saw a tiny, fluffy white kitten with four little black feet sitting on the patchwork cushion. Its soft fur seemed to be glowing faintly with hundreds of tiny sparkles.

Kara frowned, puzzled. She didn't

remember Felicity or Cherry bringing a toy cat with them. 'Wow! You look so real! I wonder where you came from?' she said, starting to push herself to her feet.

The tiny kitten blinked up at her with frightened emerald-green eyes. 'I come from far away. Can you help me to hide?' it mewed.

# Chapter
★TWO★

Kara's jaw dropped and she collapsed back into a heap on to the rug. Had the kitten really just answered her? She stared at it in complete astonishment.

'Is this some kind of trick?' she gasped, whipping round to see if Felicity was peeping through the door. She struck Kara as the sort of person who might put an electrical toy on the chair to get a reaction.

The kitten pricked up its tiny white ears. It was absolutely gorgeous, with soft fuzzy fur and the biggest emerald eyes Kara had ever seen. Its four black feet made it look as if it was wearing tiny cute shoes.

'This is not a trick. I am Prince Flame. Who are you?' the kitten miaowed.

'Kara . . . Parkes,' Kara gulped, rising to her knees. 'I'm . . . at Torc House for summer camp. Did you say *Prince* Flame?' She could still hardly believe that she was actually having a conversation with a kitten.

Flame lifted his tiny chin and his emerald eyes flashed with pride. 'Yes. I am heir to the Lion Throne. But my uncle Ebony has stolen it from me and rules in my place!'

'But . . . but you're such a tiny kitten,' Kara said, her curiosity starting to get the better of her shock.

Flame sat up indignantly. 'I will show you. Stay back!' he mewed.

Before Kara could say anything there was another silver flash, so bright that she had to look away again. When Kara looked back the tiny kitten had vanished and in its place stood a majestic young white lion with glowing emerald eyes.

'Do not be afraid. I will not harm you,' Flame said in a deep velvety growl.

Kara took a deep breath and tried very hard to stay calm. 'OK! I . . . I believe you,' she stammered.

With a final blinding flash, Flame reappeared as the tiny white kitten with four black feet. 'My uncle sends his spies to find me. I must hide now. Will you help me?' he mewed, trembling all over.

Kara was still shocked from seeing Flame as his true lion self, but right now she realized that he was just an adorable frightened little kitten. She felt her soft heart melting as she leaned forward and picked him up.

As the sparks in Flame's fur faded, they tingled slightly against her fingers and left a warm glow in her hands. 'I'll look after you, don't worry . . . Oh, I've just thought, we're not allowed pets! Someone will notice if I keep you in my room. Felicity seems to have a thing about rules. She's bound to make a fuss.'

Flame snuggled against her T-shirt. 'I will use my magic so that only you may see and hear me.'

'You can do that? Wow! That's brilliant, Flame!' Kara said. 'Wait until I tell Cherry about you. I've got a feeling that she can keep a secret.'

Flame reached up and touched her cheek with a tiny, white, black-tipped paw. 'You must tell no one, Kara. Promise me,' he purred seriously.

Kara felt disappointed. This would have been such an exciting discovery to share with a new friend, but she nodded, determined to do whatever she must to keep Flame safe.

'All right. You'll be my secret,' she said, cuddling his fluffy little body.

'Thank you, Kara,' Flame purred contentedly.

'I'd better go down for tea now or the others will wonder where I am,' Kara said. She put Flame down on to the rug and quickly put her trainers on.

'Can you make yourself invisible now?'
she asked as they went out into the
corridor together.

Flame nodded. 'It is done.'

He scampered at Kara's heels as she
went downstairs in search of the
dining room. Kara felt like pinching
herself. In her wildest dreams she had
never imagined that she'd be sharing
her time at summer camp with a
magic kitten!

'Over here!' Felicity called, pointing at
an empty seat as Kara and Flame
entered the busy dining room.

As Kara went over to her, two boys
barged past. One of them, a tough-
looking boy with short, spiky hair,
deliberately knocked against her arm.

'Hey! Watch out!' Kara cried, worried
that he was going to step on Flame.

'Watch out!' the boy copied, in a silly
baby voice. Laughing, he nudged his
friend, who wore glasses. The two of
them pulled faces at Kara before joining
a group of kids on a nearby table.

Kara glanced down worriedly. 'Are
you OK, Flame?' she whispered.

'I am fine,' Flame purred softly,
looking up at her.

Still feeling annoyed with the rough
boys, Kara sat between her new dorm-
mates.

'Did that boy kick you?' Cherry asked
worriedly.

Kara shook her head. 'No, but he
almost trod on Fl . . .' She stopped,
realizing what she had been about to
say. '. . . on my foot,' she corrected
herself quickly. She was going to have
to be a lot more careful about keeping
Flame a secret!

'Those two are a pain. The big one's
called Nathan Potts and the one with
glasses is Daz Weeks. They're in
Magpies,' Felicity said. 'I saw them
getting told off for throwing screwed-
up crisp wrappers at some pigeons.'

'Charming,' Kara said. Under the

table, she felt Flame jump up into her lap. As he settled down and started purring, she stroked his soft fluffy fur.

The dining room was noisy with everyone chatting and laughing. The different groups of kids in Starlings, Magpies, Swifts and Crows all sat at their own tables. Smaller tables with the adults, helpers and organizers were dotted round the room.

Kara helped herself to tuna sandwiches. She checked that no one was watching and began passing tiny bits under the table to Flame. He munched them hungrily and as his rough little tongue licked her fingers, Kara smiled.

'Oh!' she suddenly gasped as she felt something hit her on the head.

A custard cream biscuit dropped on to Kara's shoulder and then fell on to the floor. As she twisted round to see where it had come from, Flame sat up and rested his front paws on the table to look too. Kara panicked briefly before remembering that only she could see Flame peering round the room. Another biscuit hit her on the side of her face.

'Great shot, Nathan!' Daz Weeks cried.

'Who? Me?' Nathan rolled his eyes innocently as all the Magpies laughed.

'Those two are pathetic,' Felicity said loudly.

Nathan's eyes narrowed. 'Who are you calling pathetic?' He reached for two big currant buns and drew back his arm, taking aim.

Kara began to feel a strange warm tingling feeling down her spine. She looked down to see big sparkles fizzing all over Flame's fur, and his whiskers crackling with electricity.

Kara caught her breath. Something strange was going to happen.

# Chapter
## *THREE*

Flame lifted one tiny black-tipped
paw and sent a stream of sparks
whooshing towards the Magpies' table.
As they sprinkled down on to Nathan
like a glittery shower, he sat bolt
upright and the currant buns fell from
his fingers.

Kara watched in amazement as
Nathan reached out slowly and picked

up a half-empty bowl of trifle. He lifted
the bowl up over his head and tipped it
upside down. Cream, custard and jelly
slopped out in a gloopy mess, running
down his face.

'Wicked!' Daz gave a whoop of
laughter and clapped his hands.

Nathan put down the empty bowl
and sat there staring into space with a
pyramid of cream, topped by a cherry,
decorating his head. Streamers of yellow
custard and red jelly dripped from his
shoulders.

The whole dining room erupted with
laughter. Felicity joined in and even
Cherry was helpless.

While everyone was concentrating on
Nathan, Kara glanced at Flame. 'Oh,
Flame. What have you done?' she

scolded gently, looking into his mischievous green eyes.

'I am sorry, Kara. But I thought that boy might hurt you,' Flame purred.

'Oh, well, it serves him right for almost treading on you,' she whispered, stroking his tiny ears. The sparks in Flame's fur tickled briefly as they went out and his glowing whiskers returned to normal.

Miss Cross stormed over to the Magpies' table. 'What disgraceful behaviour, Nathan Potts! That's no example to set the younger ones. And as for you, Daniel Weeks, I saw you egging him on!'

'Me? I didn't do anything!' Daz exclaimed, pushing his glasses more firmly on to his nose.

'Come with me, both of you!' Miss Cross ordered sternly.

Daz stood up. But Nathan just sat there, looking dozy. Daz nudged him. 'Hey, Nathan, come on.'

'What . . .?' Nathan rose slowly to his feet. Sticking out his tongue, he licked a dribble of trifle off his cheek before following Daz and Miss Cross.

'All right, everyone. The fun's over now!' One of the adult helpers clapped his hands for silence. 'Let's start clearing away now, please. Here at Torc House, everyone mucks in.'

Felicity looked horrified. 'I didn't know we had to actually *work*! This is more like prison camp!'

Kara felt Flame jump down. She saw him scamper over to a window sill, where he jumped up and then began to wash himself. She smiled to herself. It was going to be brilliant fun having him around.

The next day after breakfast, Kara and Flame went to check the noticeboard, where the day's activities were listed. Felicity and Cherry were already there. 'Look, it says Starlings have got hiking today and then we've got climbing, abseiling and canoeing later in the week,' Cherry said. 'Sounds like fun!'

Felicity pulled a face. 'Hiking sounds dead boring. I'm not doing it. I'll say I've forgotten to bring my trainers or something.'

Miss Cross was passing by. 'Don't worry, Felicity, we have everything you'll need for all the activities. Hiking boots, spare socks, lifejackets, you name it,' she said helpfully. 'But don't you all forget your daily chores before you go.'

Kara bit back a grin at the disgusted look on Felicity's face.

'Come on, Felicity. We're helping to muck out the stables today,' she said. 'It'll be fun!'

Felicity didn't look convinced.

As they all entered the stable yard,

Kara saw Nathan and Daz. The boys were being shown how to groom a group of big grey ponies tethered outside their stalls.

'Oh, no, I just hope those two behave themselves. They're worse when they're together,' she whispered to Flame.

'I hope so too,' Flame mewed, keeping a wary eye on them.

Some of the other Starlings and Magpies were already at work. As Kara passed the open door of the tack room, she saw girls and boys inside polishing saddles and cleaning harnesses. She and Flame followed Cherry and Felicity into the stables, where the familiar warm smell of straw and ponies greeted them.

Kara thought of Amber at home in

her stable and felt a little sad. She hoped her dad had remembered his promise to give her pony extra cuddles. A soft nudge at her ankle interrupted Kara's thoughts and she looked down to see Flame's tiny face creased in concern.

'Is something wrong, Kara?' Flame mewed softly.

'I'm OK thanks, Flame,' Kara whispered back so that Cherry and Felicity wouldn't hear. She told him about the riding accident and Amber's strained leg.

Flame's bright-green eyes twinkled with sympathy. 'Will the animal doctor be able to make her better?'

'I don't know,' Kara answered. 'It's a really bad strain. Mum and Dad have promised to let me know what the vet says.' She sighed, making an effort not to worry.

A tall red-haired young man came over to the two of them and Kara looked up expectantly. Flame's furry brow creased thoughtfully as he settled down by her feet.

'Hi, I'm Shane,' the man said to Kara

and the girls with a friendly smile.
'You'll be finding buckets, brooms and
a wheelbarrow over there. Have you
mucked out before?'

'No,' Felicity said, shuddering.

'I share a pony with my cousin. We
look after her together,' Cherry said shyly.

'*You* have a pony?' Felicity said, trying
not to look impressed.

'I'm used to looking after my pony
too,' Kara said.

'Grand. I'll leave you to it then. You
girls can be in charge of showing your
friend here what to do. I'll see you
later,' Shane said, walking away.

'You needn't think you two are going
to boss me about!' Felicity said. 'Anyway,
how hard can mucking out be? It's just
stirring a bit of old straw around.'

Kara pressed her lips together. Felicity was such a bossy know-it-all. 'Here you are then, if you think you know what to do,' she said, passing her a fork.

Felicity tossed back her long hair and began jabbing half-heartedly at a pile of clean straw. Kara and Cherry left her to it. They set to work forking wet straw and droppings into a wheelbarrow.

'Ugh! It smells awful. How often do you have to do this?' Felicity complained loudly, wrinkling her nose, as the soiled straw began heaping up in the barrow.

'Every day. Sometimes twice in bad weather,' Kara said.

'And I don't think it smells too bad. You get used to it,' Cherry said.

'You must have something wrong

with your nose!' Felicity decided, putting down her fork and standing with her hands in her pockets. As soon as Kara and Cherry had filled the barrow she darted forward and grabbed the handles. 'I'll empty this,' she said, wheeling it outside.

Kara and Cherry went and stood in the doorway, watching as Felicity wobbled her way across to the muck heap. Flame scrabbled up the wooden door and balanced on a beam near Kara.

As Felicity drew level to Nathan, Kara saw the tough boy look up and scowl at her. Felicity stuck her tongue out at him. 'I bet you got a mega-severe telling-off, didn't you?' she crowed. 'You looked a right twerp with that trifle all over you!'

'Shut up, you!' Nathan muttered.

But Felicity didn't stop. 'I heard you lost a team point too. I bet Magpies are pleased with you. Not!'

Kara saw Nathan's ears redden and his back stiffen. She felt a warning flicker. The tough boy was bad enough without Felicity making him worse.

'Just leave it, Felicity,' she advised quietly.

'Huh! I was only sticking up for you!' Felicity said huffily, trundling past with her nose in the air.

Nathan went over to Daz and the two of them stood close, talking.

'I wonder what those two are plotting now,' Kara whispered to Flame.

Flame nodded, his eyes narrowing suspiciously.

Kara and Cherry went back into the
stables. After sweeping up they spread
clean straw in the stalls. Felicity
wheeled the empty barrow back inside
and then slouched against the door,
examining her nails, as Kara and Cherry
worked.

'Hey! Aren't you going to help?' Kara
asked.

Felicity shrugged. 'What's the point?

You two are doing fine by yourselves.'

Kara didn't trust herself to answer. She finished making the ponies a clean bed in double-quick time. 'Phew! That's about it,' she puffed, pushing back a strand of damp hair.

Shane came over just as they had finished. 'That's a grand job, girls. Well done,' he said nodding.

'Piece of cake!' Felicity chimed up, quickly standing up straight. 'Come on, you two. I'm off to get ready for hiking.'

Kara and Cherry looked at each other in disbelief. 'She is *so* annoying,' Cherry murmured.

Hiking might not be top of Kara's favourite-things-to-do list, but she had to admit that the views from the top of the windswept mountains were pretty amazing. Flame seemed to think so too.

He had jumped out of her shoulder bag and sat looking at the flocks of sheep, on the bright-green slopes below them. They looked like tiny specks of cotton wool.

'Wow! Look over there,' Kara said, pointing to some circular, hump-shaped buildings, with stone walls and ditches round them. 'How old are they?'

Flame bounded up on to the roof of the nearest building and stood there with his head in the air. The wind ruffled his fluffy white fur as he snuffled the exciting smells.

'These must be about a million years old,' Cherry said, peering into the low stone doorway. 'Imagine living up here in the middle of nowhere!'

'You must be joking!' Felicity said with a shudder. 'I bet there are huge hairy spiders in there!'

Kara nodded, agreeing with Felicity for once. 'And it hasn't even got a TV!' she joked.

Cherry and Felicity laughed.

Kara could see Nathan and Daz messing about and laughing as they jumped off a low stone wall. She kept expecting them to come over, but when they ignored her and her friends, she began to relax. Kara sighed. *I'm probably worrying about nothing*, she told herself.

# Chapter
# *FOUR*

On the way back in the minibus one of
the adult helpers started a sing-song and
everyone joined in. Nathan kept singing
the wrong words and collapsing into
giggles. Kara couldn't help laughing too.
Nathan was really quite funny when he
wasn't being mean.

Back at Torc House, Kara and Cherry
took cool drinks outside into the

grounds. Felicity went upstairs to fetch Marvin before coming back to join them on the lawn.

She sat down and cradled Marvin in the crook of her arm. 'Here we are!' She put her can of drink to the scruffy little teddy's stitched mouth. 'That's it, slurp, slurp. Lovely,' she crooned, pretending to give Marvin a drink.

'That is *so* soppy,' Cherry commented.

Felicity ignored her.

Kara grinned as she turned on to her stomach and sipped her lemonade. Flame was stretched out beside her, taking a nap. His tiny ears twitched and his little black tipped paws flexed as he dreamed.

He looked so cute that Kara had to concentrate on not reaching out and

stroking him in case Cherry and
Felicity wondered what she was doing.

'Who's making supper tonight? I'm
starving,' Cherry asked after a while.

'You can't be! The snacks you carry
around would feed about two hundred
people!' Felicity snorted.

'Oh, ha, ha,' Cherry said.

Kara hardly heard them. She was
thinking about Amber again. She hoped
that her sore leg wasn't hurting her too
much.

As Flame stirred and sat up yawning,
Kara rose to her feet. 'I think I'll phone
home and see if the vet's been to see
Amber yet,' she decided.

Felicity jumped to her feet too. 'And
I'm going to take Marvin back upstairs.
He wants a nap now.'

Cherry watched Felicity go, shaking her head in disbelief, but smiling too. 'It's kind of sweet that she's so fond of that scruffy old teddy, isn't it?'

Kara nodded and smiled back.

Kara's mum answered on the third ring. 'Hello, love. I was just about to ring you. Are you having a good time?'

Kara said that she was, and excitedly

told her mum about sharing with Felicity and Cherry and going hiking. She didn't think she should mention Flame, who was sitting invisibly at her ankles!

'Has the vet been to see Amber, Mum?'

'Yes. He's only just left,' Mrs Parkes said. 'There's not much to tell, I'm afraid. He still doesn't know if Amber's leg will heal properly. It's a matter of time.'

Kara felt a lump rising in her throat. 'But what if it never gets better? I might never be able to ride her again.' She gulped.

'You mustn't think like that, love. Let's just wait and see,' her mum said gently. 'Amber's young and healthy.'

Kara's spirits were flat as she said goodbye and put down the phone. Flame wound himself around her ankles, rubbing against her sympathetically.

'I am sorry that you feel bad for Amber,' he purred softly.

'Thanks, Flame,' Kara said, reaching down to stroke him. She didn't feel like going to find Cherry and Felicity just yet. She wandered back up to the girls' dorm to be by herself for a while.

Flame scampered along beside her.

As they got closer, Kara saw that the door to their room was wide open. 'That's odd,' she said, puzzled.

Flame pricked up his ears. 'There is someone inside.'

Kara frowned as she moved closer

until she too could hear muffled
laughter.

'Quick! Someone's outside!' a familiar
voice called out.

Two boys shot out. They ignored
Kara and headed away without a
backward glance. She heard their foot-
steps thudding down the back stairs.

'Hey, stop! That was Nathan and Daz!'
Kara cried. She rushed into the dorm.
'Oh, no!' she gasped.

All the pillows, duvets and sheets had
been dragged off the beds and piled up
into a heap in the middle of the room.
But that wasn't all. Her eyes widened in
dismay as she realized that everything
was soaking wet.

'I *knew* they were planning something.
We'll never get that lot dry!' Kara said,

clenc

enoug

Flam

'Do no

Kara 1

her spine

with silve

crackled w

She watc ...c pointed a paw
and sent a fountain of silver sparks
towards the big pile of bedding. The
sparks whipped into a sparkling tornado
which spun faster and faster until it
was just a glittering whirr before Kara's
eyes. The tornado zoomed all over the
bedding, sucking up every last drop
of water like a magic hoover, before
whizzing towards the nearby open
window.

*Magic Kitten*

The spinning silv

as it squeezed t

once outsi

in mid

to

er tornado flattened

hrough the window and

e, the whole thing dissolved

-air. Water poured down in a

rent, just as if someone had tipped it

out of a huge bucket.

'Aargh!' shrieked a voice from below.

'Help, I'm soaked,' cried another one.

Kara dashed to the window and stuck her head outside.

Nathan and Daz stood there drenched
to the skin. They must have been
waiting outside, gloating about their
mean trick – just in time to get caught
in the downpour.

A laugh bubbled up in Kara's throat.
'Oops! Bad luck!' she shouted.

Nathan glanced up. His face twisted.
'You threw that water on purpose. We'll
get you for that!' he yelled.

'I'd say we were even. Wouldn't you?'
Kara crowed as Nathan and Daz
squelched away. She was still giggling
when she pulled her head back inside.
'That's showed those two! Thanks again,
Flame!'

But Flame hadn't finished yet. He
pointed his little black paw at the
crumpled pile of bedding and another

jet of silver sparks shot out.

Phwit! The whole pile of bedding jumped in the air and shook out their creases. Rustle! They divided into three sets and marched in formation to the beds like a line of soldiers. Phloop! The sheet fitted itself on the mattress, the pillow plumped itself up and the duvet did a quick shimmy and settled back into place.

Kara clapped her hands with delight. Scooping Flame up she kissed the top of his fuzzy little head. 'Wow! That was amazing!' she said.

Flame purred and rubbed his face against her arm affectionately. 'I am glad I could help.'

She was still sitting on the bed cuddling Flame when Felicity and

Cherry came in. Kara quickly sat up, thinking how odd it would look if she seemed to be holding an empty space.

Felicity marched straight up, grinning all over her face. 'So it's true! It was you!'

Kara frowned. 'What was me?'

'Nathan and Daz just came into the games room soaking wet,' Cherry explained. 'They said you leaned out of the window and chucked water all over them.'

'Well, did you?' Felicity demanded.

'Yes, I did . . .' Kara said and then she stopped. How was she going to explain what had happened? She couldn't tell them about the soaked beds because then she'd have to explain how Flame had magically made them up again. 'I did it because I . . . um, felt like it!'

'Good for you. I wish I'd seen their faces!' Cherry said, chuckling.

Suddenly Felicity pointed at her bed and gave a loud shriek.

Kara and Cherry almost jumped out of their skins. 'What?' they chorused.

'It's Marvin. He's gone!' Felicity said, horrified.

Kara looked over at her bed, where the old teddy was usually propped up against the pillow. It was true. Marvin was nowhere in sight. 'Maybe he's fallen on to the floor. I'm sure he must be here somewhere.'

'Kara's right. I'll help you look,' Cherry said.

Between them they searched every bit of the room. Cherry even looked right under the bed and Kara helped Felicity pull out the chests of drawers so they could look in the narrow space behind them. But they didn't find Marvin.

Kara looked across at Flame, who was nosing around helpfully trying to sniff out the teddy. An awful suspicion was dawning on her. 'I think I know who's taken him,' she whispered.

But Felicity had worked it out for herself. 'Nathan and Daz have stolen him! And they won't give him back after what Kara just did to them. I'm never going to see Marvin again!' She rounded on Kara and her mouth twisted as she burst into noisy sobs. 'It's all *your* fault! I hate you!'

# Chapter
# *FIVE*

Kara looked at Felicity in utter dismay.
How come she felt like a horrid
criminal, when it wasn't even her fault?

She went over and put her arm
round Felicity's shoulder. 'Look, I'm
really sorry about Marvin. Come on.
Let's go and tell Miss Cross what's
happened.'

'No, don't!' Felicity gulped. 'Nathan's

not going to admit what he's done. And if we snitch on him, he . . . he could hurt Marvin.'

'She's got a point,' Cherry said. 'It would be just like him to cut Marvin into tiny bits and flush him down the loo . . .' She faltered as Felicity gave an extra-loud wail. 'Sorry.'

'Right,' Kara said, thinking out loud. 'Nathan's going to expect us to make a fuss about Marvin, isn't he? How about if we don't mention him and we pretend we don't care . . .'

'Don't care! Of all the heartless —' Felicity began.

'No, listen,' Kara urged. 'We only *pretend* we don't. Of course we're all dead worried about poor old Marvin, aren't we, Cherry?'

'Er . . . yeah,' Cherry said.

'OK, think about it, right? Nathan won't be able to resist crowing about pinching Marvin, will he? He'll probably hold him to ransom for a huge bar of chocolate or something. And then we'll have a chance of getting him back!' Kara reasoned.

Felicity blinked tearfully. 'Do you think so?'

'Oh, yes. No doubt about it,' Kara said, sounding more confident that she felt. She dreaded to think how Felicity would react if Marvin was never seen again.

'Well, OK then,' Felicity sniffled. 'But I jolly well hope you're right.'

Over the next few days, Kara and Cherry made a huge effort to cheer Felicity up.

Felicity seemed to enjoy herself when Starlings went abseiling and then on a trip to a nearby funfair. But every night she just got into bed and pulled the duvet over her head, sniffling into her pillow.

'I don't know what to say to her,' Kara whispered to Flame in the dark.

She knew that Felicity was lying there awake, missing Marvin like mad. Felicity could be maddening but she felt really sorry for her. 'Is there something you could do to help her feel better?'

'Magic can fix lots of things, but it cannot change people's feelings,' Flame mewed sadly.

The following morning, Kara and Flame, Felicity and Cherry and the other Starlings were doing recycling as their daily chore.

'The first week's gone by really quickly, hasn't it?' Cherry said, packing plastic bottles into a large container for collection.

Kara nodded, using a small hand-held crusher to squash drinks cans into tin discs. Flame watched in fascination, skipping sideways and play-growling as each can collapsed with a crackling sound. Kara smiled at his playful antics. Sometimes it was hard to remember that the cute kitten was a prince in his own world.

'I'm glad *you're* having fun,' Felicity said moodily to Kara, catching her smiling to herself. She stamped hard on a small cardboard box to flatten it. 'Your brilliant plan to pretend we don't care about Marvin was useless. Nathan's got

no intention of ever giving him back.
Have you got any more fantastic ideas?'

Kara bit her lip, feeling awful. 'Um . . .
not really.'

'That's what I thought,' Felicity
grumbled. 'Thanks for nothing.'

After chores were finished Starlings
had wall-climbing up the side of
Torc House. Wearing a safety harness
and helmet Kara grasped the special

hand-holds to scale the wall and reach a wooden platform.

Flame bounded up beside her, jumping from place to place like a mountain goat. 'This is great fun!' he mewed, giving Kara a whiskery grin.

Kara really enjoyed it too but the problem of Marvin was still on her mind.

'I don't get it,' she said to Flame in the bathroom as she brushed her teeth that night. 'Why haven't Nathan and Daz teased Felicity about pinching Marvin or asked her to buy him back or something?' She sighed deeply. 'It's not their style to just keep him. Maybe we're wrong and they haven't got him.'

Flame's bright-green eyes were thoughtful. 'No. I think that you are right about those boys, Kara. I have a strong feeling that they are planning something.'

'Well, we'll just have to wait and see, I suppose,' Kara said. 'It's canoeing tomorrow. That should be good and maybe it'll take Felicity's mind off Marvin.'

Kara stood by the river with the other Starlings as she fastened the straps on her lifejacket. The morning sun gleamed on the flowing water. Jewelled dragonflies flashed back and forth, hunting for flies.

She saw Felicity staring up the river-bank to where the Magpies were getting into canoes. Nathan and Daz were laughing and jostling each other as usual.

'Don't think about them. They're not worth it,' Kara said.

'That's easy for you to say,' Felicity said.

Kara sighed as she climbed into the large canoe beside Cherry. Flame jumped in after her, settling himself under Kara's seat and purring happily. Once the canoe was full everyone picked up their oars and began to row.

Kara rowed in time with Cherry as the canoe floated smoothly downriver.

'This is great, isn't it?' Cherry said, pulling on her oar.

Everyone's oars splashed in time and now and then a moorhen's call echoed across the water. Flame crawled out from under the seat. He stood up on his back paws and curled his front paw

over the canoe's rim to peer curiously
into the water.

'Be careful you don't fall in,' Kara
whispered.

The Magpies' canoe drew level with
the Starlings' and then began to
overtake them. Kara saw Nathan
quickly lean over and put something
into the water.

It was a small paper boat. Kara watched it floating towards her, bobbing up and down in the water. Propped up in it was a tiny familiar figure.

'Marvin! He's in that paper boat!' Felicity screeched. She let go of her oar and leapt to her feet.

As Felicity stumbled backwards, the canoe rocked and then dipped low to one side. Kara leaned forward and grabbed at Flame, but her fingers closed on empty space. He gave a wail of alarm and there was a tiny splash as Flame disappeared under the water.

# Chapter
## *SIX*

'Hey! Where did that kitten come from?' Cherry cried, pointing at the water as Flame's tiny head surfaced.

'Oh, no!' Kara gasped. Everyone could see Flame!

The shock of hitting the cold water must have made him forget to be invisible. Now he couldn't use his magic to save himself without giving himself away!

Kara could see Flame's tiny legs
moving frantically under the water.
Would he be able to make it across the
river? The opposite bank seemed an
awfully long way away.

Suddenly she noticed that the
Magpies' canoe was heading straight for
Flame! They couldn't see him in the
choppy water. 'Look out for that kitten!'
she screamed, her heart racing.

But the Magpies hadn't seen him and
their canoe was moving fast, closing in
on Flame with every second. He would
never be able to swim clear in time.

Kara didn't think twice. She leapt up
out of her seat and jumped straight into
the water. There was a huge splash and
the cold took her breath away but she
bobbed up at once and her lifejacket

kept her afloat. Gasping, she kicked out
strongly towards Flame and the canoe
that was bearing down on him.

'Girl overboard!' Cherry shouted.

'There's the kitten!' someone shouted
from the Magpies' canoe.

Kara recognized the voice. It was Nathan. She had a quick glance at his shocked white face as he pulled hard on one oar. The canoe swerved, just enough to miss Flame by a few centimetres. The wash from the Magpies' canoe swept Flame further away from Kara.

She kicked out harder as she saw that Flame's movements were getting weaker. The cold must be sapping his strength. Closer, closer. Almost there. She gave a final desperate lunge. Yes! She reached out and grabbed Flame by the scruff of his neck.

'Got you!' she cried. 'You're safe now.'

Flame coughed and spat out river water. Scrabbling up her lifejacket, he clung to her shoulder, shivering and whimpering.

As Kara struck out towards the bank with Flame, all the kids in the canoes started cheering and waving. She swam one-handed and waved back to show she was all right.

A soggy object, already half under water, drifted near her hand.

The paper boat with Marvin inside!

On impulse, Kara scooped it up and stuffed it into the top of her lifejacket. A few minutes later she reached shallow water. She waded through the muddy reeds and climbed out of the river. Finally she flopped down to catch her breath.

Flame jumped down on to the grass beside her. He looked even smaller than usual, with his wet fur plastered to his tiny body. He placed a tiny, black-tipped paw on her arm and blinked up at her with bright emerald eyes. 'Thank you for saving me. You were very brave, Kara,' he purred.

She smiled down at him fondly. 'I wasn't really. I just couldn't bear to see you in danger.' It was true, she realized. She hated to think of anything happening to her friend.

'Kara! Are you all right?' Miss Cross called, steering the Starlings' canoe into the bank. Felicity, Cherry and the other Starlings all jumped on to the grass and helped drag the canoe out of the water.

'Quick! You'd better hide until they've gone. Otherwise they'll make a big fuss and try to find out who you belong to!' Kara whispered to Flame.

Flame nodded. With a swish of his tail he darted into the nearby reeds.

Miss Cross stormed up the bank with
Felicity and Cherry close behind her.

'Uh-oh! Now I'm for it,' Kara
breathed.

'Whatever possessed you to jump in,
you silly girl?' Miss Cross scolded. 'It
was a very dangerous thing to do! You
almost capsized the canoe and had us
all in the water!'

'Er . . . um . . .' Kara stammered,
playing for time. She leaned forward as
she rose to her feet and the soggy
paper boat and teddy tipped out of her
lifejacket and fell on to the grass.

'Marvin!' Felicity shrieked, swooping
down to grab her teddy. 'I thought he'd
gone forever.' She turned shining eyes
on Kara. 'Thank you so much for
saving him! I'll never forget this,' she

said, and then her face became serious. 'Leave this to me,' she whispered, turning to Miss Cross. 'It was my fault, Miss,' she said in a louder voice. 'When I saw Nathan put poor Marvin in that paper boat I was so shocked that I stood up. That's when the canoe almost overturned and Kara fell out.'

'Fell out? But, I saw Kara jump in . . .' Miss Cross said, looking puzzled.

Felicity widened her blue eyes innocently. 'Oh, no, Miss. It might have looked like that, but she definitely fell in. You ask Cherry. She was nearest to Kara.'

'Felicity's right, Miss. I saw everything,' Cherry said firmly.

'Well, perhaps I was mistaken. It all happened so fast. What about that kitten? Did anyone see what happened to it?' Miss Cross asked.

'I . . . er, think it ran off. It . . . was probably . . . a stray. Brrr–rrr–rr.' Kara's teeth started to chatter. She hugged herself to try and stop shivering.

'Oh, dear. You'd best get out of those wet clothes before you catch cold,' Miss Cross said, looking concerned. 'I'll drive you back to Torc House. The rest of you, wait here for me, please. I'll be back as soon as I can.'

As Kara climbed into the minibus and sat down, Flame jumped on to the seat next to her, purring loudly.

Twenty minutes later, Kara was drying herself after a long hot shower. Flame sat on the bath mat, waiting for her.

Kara pulled on a bathrobe. 'That's better. I feel like a new person.' Picking Flame up, she cuddled him and then wrinkled her nose. 'Phew! Muddy river water! How do you fancy a bath in the sink?'

'No, thank you. I have already been wet today!' Flame mewed indignantly.

'Yes, and excuse me for saying so, but

you don't half pong!' Kara said. 'Come on. It won't take long and then I'll dry you with the hairdryer. You'll like that.' Flame looked down his tiny nose doubtfully. 'I am not sure that I will. But, very well, I trust your word.'

Kara bathed him gently, taking great care to keep shower gel well away from his eyes and ears. She rinsed him in warm water and then blotted him with a towel. 'Let's go into the bedroom. There's no one in there.'

Flame sat on Kara's lap as she switched the hairdryer on to a low setting. At first he tensed at the unfamiliar noise and laid his ears back, but he gradually relaxed as the warm air ruffled his fur.

'Nice?' Kara asked.

Flame gave a hesitant purr. 'It feels very strange but I quite like it.'

Kara smiled, wondering if anyone else had ever bathed a lion prince! 'There,' she said a few minutes later as she put the hairdryer away. 'Now you're all dry and you smell gorgeous.' *And you look like a fuzzy ball of cotton wool*, she thought, swallowing a giggle in case she hurt his pride.

Flame jumped on to her bed and pedalled the duvet into a soft nest. Kara curled herself round him. She only intended to relax for a few minutes but it was almost two hours later when Felicity and Cherry came bursting in.

'Guess what! Nathan and Daz have lost more team points *and* they've been grounded,' Cherry said.

Kara sat up rubbing her eyes. 'Really?' she said, quickly shifting so that she sat in front of the tiny dent Flame made.

'Yeah, they have to stay inside Torc House tomorrow and miss out on the barbecue in the grounds,' Felicity said gleefully. 'I think they should have been grounded for about ten years after what they did to Marvin!' She held up the tattered teddy, which looked even more bedraggled than usual after his soaking.

Kara smiled as Felicity exaggerated as usual. But at least Felicity was happy again and they might all get a good night's sleep.

# Chapter
## *SEVEN*

'Why is it that time passes so quickly when you're having a good time?' Kara said to Flame as she changed out of her sports kit a few days later.

Flame shook his head. 'I do not know but I have noticed this too,' he purred.

Kara had just finished a tennis match. Starlings had been playing against

Magpies, and Magpies had won by two sets to one.

Cherry and Felicity came into the changing rooms. 'Nathan's a great player. I really enjoyed the match,' Cherry commented, wiping her forehead with the back of her hand. 'He's actually a real laugh when he's not being mean.'

Kara nodded. She had noticed that too. Nathan and Daz had been on their best behaviour for days now. Maybe they had really learned their lesson this time. And Kara remembered it was Nathan calling out that had made the Magpies turn their canoe in time to miss hitting Flame.

'Only two days left now. I thought I'd really miss home but now I wish I was

stopping here for a month,' Felicity said
glumly.

'At least there's the group pony trek
to look forward to. I can't wait to go
riding,' Cherry said.

'Me too. I haven't been riding since
Amber hurt her leg,' Kara said. She had
spoken to her parents the previous
evening, but there was no more news
about Amber.

'I'm sorry about Amber,' Felicity said unexpectedly. She came over and put an arm round Kara's and Cherry's shoulders. 'I know I can be a pain but you've both been really nice to me. Shall we promise to keep in touch when we get home?' she asked.

Kara was touched. She looked over at Cherry. Cherry blushed, looking really pleased.

'Deal!' they chorused.

The following day, Kara peered out of the dorm window at the sunlit mountains. The slopes looked fresh and bright and the peaks showed greyish purple against the blue sky.

'Look, Flame. It's a purr-fect day for pony trekking!' she joked.

Flame didn't answer, but gave a muffled little miaow.

Kara turned back to her bed in surprise. Usually he was up and about by now, his tiny face alight with anticipation, but today he was still buried deep beneath the duvet.

'Come on, sleepyhead. Time to go,' she urged, digging a hand under the duvet and tickling him gently. 'I need to go and get into my riding gear. Cherry and Felicity have already gone.'

Flame poked his head out, revealing dull fur and flattened ears. His whiskers quivered as his whole body trembled. 'I cannot come with you, Kara.'

Kara froze, her teasing smile fading. 'What's wrong? Do you feel poorly?'

Flame shook his head. 'I sense my enemies drawing near.'

'Oh, no!' Alarm shot through Kara's body. She had almost convinced herself that this day would never come. Now it was here. And Flame was in terrible danger. 'What can I do to help you? Shall I stay here with you?'

'No. It is better if you go riding with the others. So many ponies moving

about on the mountain may confuse
my uncle's spies.'

Kara nodded slowly. What Flame said
made sense but she hated to leave him.
He seemed so tiny and vulnerable. 'But
I might never see you again or . . . or
get the chance to say goodbye,' she said
hesitantly.

'I will find you later, if I can,' Flame
promised, looking up at her with
troubled emerald eyes, before turning
and crawling back under the duvet.

Kara desperately wanted to pick him
up and cuddle him better but she
knew she had to be very brave and
leave him there as he had asked. She
took a deep breath and went out
quickly. 'Good luck, Flame,' she said in
a small, trembling voice. 'Please take

care and I really, really hope I'll see you later.'

The stable yard was heaving with Starlings, Swifts, Crows, Magpies and adult helpers as everyone mounted their ponies.

Kara swung her leg over Shamrock, and sat down in the saddle. She was trying hard not to think about Flame and to look forward to the day's trekking.

'Are you all right?' Cherry asked from her pony, Flossie.

Felicity's pony was called Daisy. She looked over and smiled at Kara. 'I just know Amber's going to be fine,' she said.

'Thanks,' Kara said, wishing she could

tell her friends that she was more worried about Flame right now. As she imagined the fierce cats combing the mountain slopes for a scent of their tiny royal prey, a shiver ran down her back.

'Lead the way, Starlings!' called Miss Cross from her bay horse.

Cherry, Felicity and Kara moved their ponies forward and the long line of ponies made their way up the mountain track.

As they rose higher, Kara could see the blue lakes and colourful woodland of the national park spreading out far below her. Shamrock was a lovely gentle pony and moved very smoothly up the steep tracks. Kara wished she could enjoy it all much more than she was able to right now.

When everyone dismounted for a picnic, Kara sat with Cherry, Felicity and the other Starlings. Everyone else seemed to be chatting and enjoying the warm sunshine. But as Kara remounted Shamrock, she noticed that clouds were gathering.

They had barely begun the return journey when a mist began to descend. Within minutes the mountains tops were blanked out.

'Keep close together, everyone,' Miss Cross called from up front. 'We don't want anyone to become separated.'

*At least Flame's enemies should have a hard job to find him too*, Kara thought hopefully. She peered ahead as Shamrock picked her way steadily down the track. 'That's it, girl. Steady now.'

'I don't like this. It's a bit spooky, isn't it?' Felicity said beside her.

Kara nodded. It was amazing how different everything looked. On the way up the mountains were bright and friendly. Now the trees made mysterious shapes and the ponies and riders ahead of them were smudges of shadow.

'The mist's still getting thicker. I can hardly see four metres in front of me now,' Kara said worriedly. Suddenly a cry and a snort of alarm came from behind her. She halted Shamrock and turned in the saddle. 'What's wrong?'

'It's Flossie! She's refusing to go on. I can't get her to budge,' Cherry called worriedly.

Kara carefully turned Shamrock and rode up to Cherry. 'Give me Flossie's reins. I'll try leading her,' she suggested.

'Good idea,' Cherry said.

Kara held Flossie's reins and urged Shamrock forward slowly, but Flossie whinnied and dug in her heels. 'It's no good. I think she's spooked by the mist.'

'Hey! What's the hold-up? You're blocking the way!' Nathan called, halting beside Kara and Cherry. Daz was close behind him.

'It's Flossie. She won't move. Maybe she's cast a shoe or something,' Kara explained.

'No problem. We'll ride down and tell Miss Cross and the others. There's a short cut down here. I saw it on the way up. Come on, Daz!' Nathan said.

'No, don't go off the track!' Kara said in alarm. 'You'll get lost.'

Nathan squared his shoulders. 'No way! I know what I'm doing.'

As Nathan and Daz steered their ponies down the slope, Flossie gave a sudden lurch forward after them and pulled her reins out of Kara's hands. Cherry wobbled, almost losing her balance and then leaned forward and wrapped her arms round Flossie's neck.

'Cherry!' Felicity cried. 'Come on, Daisy, after her!'

Kara had no choice. She squeezed Shamrock on and followed the others, hoping like mad that Nathan knew where he was going. The thick mist had muffled all sound and it left fine droplets on the ponies' manes.

Suddenly pony shapes seemed to loom up at Kara. 'Oh,' she gasped, just managing to stop before she rode into Nathan, Daz, Cherry and Felicity. 'What's wrong? Why've you all stopped?'

'Because we're lost, that's why!' Felicity said. 'Admit it, Nathan. Your fat-headed idea about taking a short cut was rubbish!'

'OK. But I was just trying to help! It wasn't *my* pony that had a stressy, was it?' Nathan snapped back.

'It's no use arguing,' Kara said quickly before a row broke out. 'We have to decide what to do.'

'Kara's right. We can't see a thing in this mist. There could be a steep drop just metres away,' Cherry said.

'Don't be daft,' Nathan said, but Kara thought he sounded worried.

'Look, once the mist clears, we'll be able to see where we are,' Kara reasoned, sounding calmer than she felt.

'But what if it doesn't?' Felicity gulped. 'I'm already cold and I don't fancy staying up here all night.'

*Me neither*, Kara thought.

She shivered and fought a sudden wave of panic. If only Flame was here. He'd be able to help. But Flame had to fight his own battle, hiding from his uncle. It looked like they were by themselves.

# Chapter
# *EIGHT*

Kara stood beside a large rock, holding Shamrock's reins. Cherry, Felicity, Daz and Nathan had also dismounted. They stood close together in silence, thinking about what they should do.

The clammy mist swirled around them and now the light was fading. 'Easy, girl,' Kara said reassuringly, stroking Shamrock's cheek as the pony shifted nervously. She wasn't looking forward to a cold, dark, scary night on the mountain.

Suddenly, out of nowhere, a tiny glowing shape appeared on top of the rock. Kara felt a furry head rubbing against her cold hand and then a rough little tongue licked her fingers.

'Flame!' she whispered delightedly. 'You're safe! I didn't think I'd ever see you again.'

'I told you I would find you if I could. My enemies have passed by. But if they come back, I will have to leave at once,' he mewed softly.

Kara beamed at him. 'I'm just so glad you're here now!' she whispered. 'We're lost and it's cold and almost dark. There's no way we can risk getting down.'

Flame's eyes brightened thoughtfully. 'I will be back soon,' he purred, leaping into the mist and disappearing. He was back almost at once. 'I have found somewhere for you all to shelter. Follow me,' he urged, beckoning with a fluffy front paw.

Kara looked across at the others.
'OK, everyone. I've er . . . just
remembered seeing a map of the
mountain back at Torc House. If we
go this way, we'll find shelter,' she said,
pointing to where Flame was glowing
softly in the mist.

Nathan looked suspicious. 'What map?
I've never seen one.'

'Who cares? If no one's got a better
idea, I'm going after Kara,' Felicity said.

'So am I,' Cherry said.

'Me too. Come on, Nathan. It's dead
creepy here,' Daz urged.

Kara led the small procession after
Flame, keeping her eyes on his tiny
sparkling form as he scampered up the
steep slope. Barely five minutes passed
before a dark shape loomed out of the

mist and Shamrock almost stumbled through a gap in a low stone wall.

'It's OK, everyone. Here it is!' Kara called over her shoulder.

Kara realized that they had found the old stone buildings from where they'd been hiking the other day. She saw Flame run inside the smallest of them. As Kara tethered Shamrock a familiar warm prickling tickled her spine. While the others were seeing to their ponies, she quickly followed Flame inside.

She saw sparks ignite in Flame's fur and his whiskers fizzle with power. He lifted a tiny paw and sent a whoosh of sparks zooming round the stone hut.

Snap! A rusty old lamp on a hook lit up by itself. Crackle! A small fire appeared in the fireplace. Rustle and thud! Firewood piled itself up neatly and a layer of clean dry bracken spread itself across the floor.

The very last sparks had just faded from Flame's coat when Felicity came in. 'Wow! It's really cosy in here,' she said, looking impressed. 'How did you light the fire and stuff, Kara?'

'Mum taught me survival skills. She used to be in the Guides,' Kara fibbed.

Nathan, Daz and Cherry also looked around in amazement as they came in. Cherry investigated a dusty stone shelf. 'Look, tin cups and a pot of water. It smells fresh. It should be OK if we boil it.'

'Boiled water, delicious,' Nathan said, pulling a face.

Cherry grinned and dug into her backpack. 'How about hot chocolate, crisps and ginger biscuits all round?'

Nathan cheered and Kara joined in with a grin.

Felicity gave Cherry a hug. 'You're a star! I'll never tease you about carrying snacks around again!' she promised.

Daz suddenly remembered his mobile phone. He rang Torc House to tell everyone they were safe, before settling down. 'They know where we are.

Someone's coming to get us as soon as the mist clears,' he told them.

An hour later, after they'd eaten, everyone curled up on the dry bracken. Cherry, Felicity, Nathan and Daz fell asleep straightaway, but Kara lay awake cuddling Flame.

'Thanks again for coming to find me. You're the most brilliant friend ever,' she whispered sleepily.

'You are welcome, Kara,' Flame purred, and snuggled against her.

Kara fell asleep with her cheek against Flame's soft fur. When she woke, the lantern was low and it was dark inside the little hut. As she stirred, she felt Flame stiffen and then leap out of her arms. She opened her eyes just in time to see him bounding out of the door.

'Flame?'

With suspicion rising up in her, she got up and quietly went outside after him. Suddenly, from the pitch-black night came a blinding silver flash. The tethered ponies twitched their ears, but none of them made a sound.

Kara blinked hard as her sight cleared. Flame stood there as his magnificent real self. Sparks gleamed in the majestic young white lion's dazzling coat and his emerald eyes glowed. An older grey lion with a wise face stood next to Flame.

And then Kara knew that this time Flame was leaving for good.

'Your enemies are very close. We must go,' the grey lion rumbled.

Flame raised a huge white paw in

farewell. 'Be well, Kara,' he said in a
deep velvety purr.

Kara's throat closed with tears and
there was an ache in her chest.
'Goodbye, Flame,' she whispered
hoarsely. 'Take care.'

There was a final bright flash and
Flame and the older lion disappeared.

Kara glimpsed the sinister outline of his uncle's spies against the dark night and heard a shriek of rage before they too disappeared.

There was a sound behind her and Cherry, Felicity, Nathan and Daz came tumbling outside. 'What's happening?' Felicity murmured sleepily. 'Are you OK? We heard voices.'

'Kara? Felicity?' Miss Cross's head appeared above the low stone wall and a beam of torchlight swung towards them. 'And Nathan and Daz too. Here they all are, safe and sound!' she called to someone over her shoulder and then she turned back with a frown. 'I think someone has some serious explaining to do! But first,' she said with a twinkle in her eye, 'I've got a message for you,

Kara. Your parents phoned just before we left. They said to tell you that the vet says Amber's leg is almost better. It's healed like magic.'

'Really?' Kara gasped.

Somehow she knew that this was Flame's final gift to her. A dart of pure joy seemed to pierce her sadness. 'Thank you so much, Flame. I'll never forget you,' she whispered.

She couldn't wait to go home and make a big fuss of Amber and tell her all about her exciting adventures with her magical friend!

# Win a Magic Kitten goody bag!

An urgent and secret message has been left for Flame from his own world, where his evil uncle is still hunting for him.

Two words from the message can be found in royal lion crowns hidden in *Seaside Mystery* and *Firelight Friends*. Find the hidden words and put them together to complete the message. Send it in to us and each month we will put every correct message in a draw and pick out one lucky winner who will receive a purrfect Magic Kitten gift!

Send your secret message, name and address on a postcard to:

Magic Kitten Competition

Puffin Books

80 Strand

London WC2R 0RL

# Hurry, Flame needs your help!

## Good luck!

Visit:
penguin.co.uk/static/cs/uk/0/competition/terms.html
for full terms and conditions

puffin.co.uk

## Seaside Mystery

### Flame needs to find a purrfect new friend!

And that's how Maisie's
lonely new seaside life
becomes a real splash when
she rescues frightened
brown tabby kitten Flame . . .

# Coming Soon . . .

A Christmas Surprise
978–0–141–32323–7

puffin.co.uk